SO-BRA-902

Under the
Pear Tree

Under the Pear Tree

Brenda Seabrooke

Illustrated by Roger Essley

COBBLEHILL BOOKS/Dutton • New York

FRANKLIN PIERCE
COLLEGE LIBRARY
RINDGE, N.H. 03461

Text copyright © 1997 by Brenda Seabrooke
Illustrations copyright © 1997 by Roger Essley
All rights reserved. No part of this book may be reproduced in any
form without permission in writing from the Publisher.

Library of Congress Cataloging-in-Publication Data
Seabrooke, Brenda.
Under the pear tree / Brenda Seabrooke ; illustrated by Roger Essley.
p.   cm.
Summary: A collection of narrative poems about three girls growing
up in the South during the 1950s and what happens when they dis-
cover boys.
ISBN 0-525-65213-2
1. Girls—Southern States—Juvenile poetry.   2. Children's poetry,
American.   [1. American poetry.]   I. Essley, Roger, ill.   II. Title.
PS3569.E154U53   1997   811'.54—dc20   96-7461   CIP   AC

Published in the United States by Cobblehill Books,
an affiliate of Dutton Children's Books,
a division of Penguin Books USA Inc.,
375 Hudson Street, New York, New York 10014
Designed by Jean Krulis
Printed in the United States of America
First Edition   10 9 8 7 6 5 4 3 2 1

CURR
P2
7
S4376
Und
1997

To the real Avram, Davis, and Jesse—Penson Kaminsky, Franklin Sweat, and Michael Chalverus— and again to Bonnie and Andrea

The Pear Tree

That summer under
the pear tree we
discussed boys,
an exotic species
like Komodo Dragons
or Tasmanian Devils.
We lay in the island
of grass-fringed shade
and watched green, satin-backed
June bugs feasting
on fallen pears that only
grew every other year but
were twice as good as the yearly
kind. Sometimes the June bugs
walked on our arms and legs
with their needlefeet,
tickling and prickling at
the same time.

Clouds floated
overhead with all the time
in the world to get
where they were going.

The Announcement

I dropped my news
like a stone into
that pool of pear tree shade.
My cousin Rusty is coming
to visit, I said,
while his mother has a baby.
Stacy sat up. Lala
rolled over and slapped a bug
off her ankle.
He's almost thirteen, I said.
(Older than the boys in
our neighborhood.)
He's city sophisticated,
from Cincinnati, I said.
Stacy flopped back down,
Lala scratched her ankle,
and I watched the clouds.
Nobody said anything. We
weren't sure what it meant
but suddenly summer was ripe
with possibilities.

The Dog Wedding

In spring the pear tree looked
like a bride's bouquet. I dreamed
sometimes of carrying it, scaled
to fit my hands, down the aisle.
When we were little, Stacy, Lala, and I,
we had weddings
underneath the flowering tree.
We stuck pear blossoms in our hair and
tied branches together for bouquets.
We wore our mothers' discarded
nightgowns and married my dogs,
Lefty, Bebop, and Pittypat.
The dogs panted and rolled their eyes
as we marched them on their back legs
down the grassy aisle under the tree.
When we reached the orange-crate altar
we realized we had forgotten
to provide a preacher and called
time-out to find one.
Avram across the street said

in the synagogue girls didn't marry dogs,
but we thought he just didn't want
to play with us. Davis
was going fishing, *he said,*
so we were stuck with Stacy's
little brother, Jesse.
He didn't look like a preacher
in his yellow playsuit and fuzzy
yellow hair. We had to tell
him every word, so the ceremony
sounded like an echo. We were
just getting to the
I-now-pronounce-you-
husband-and-wife part when
Mrs. Hitch's cat, thinking herself
safe, sauntered down the alley between
our houses and the grooms went
after her. It was a good thing
because we didn't want to have
to kiss the dogs.

Summer Smells

Our windows were open,
our doors never locked
in the daytime except sometimes
the front screen was hooked.
Friends came in the other
three doors all day,
along with the green watermelon
flavor of fresh-mown
grass cut with a whirring
hand mower, the whoosh
of cars down Roanoke Drive,
followed by plumes of red dust
and sweet honeysuckle and other
flowery smells. Attic fans
pulled curtains inward
like long lacy streamers
and made sounds
like a giant seashell roaring
somewhere overhead.

The Tar Line

That summer men came
to pave Roanoke all
the way to Merrimac Drive.
They brought burbling asphalt
machines that burped out
the black tar and
covered the red road
forever. Jesse dipped a
stick into an oozing pool
and raced with it like
a shiny black torch
to mark a line on the sidewalk
between his house and mine.
This line will be here forever,
he shouted, as the tar cooled
and lost its shine. It became
a landmark in the games
we played at night, Redlight

and Mother, May I. When someone
was caught sneaking in the dark,
Go back to the tar line!
we shouted.

A Personal Galaxy

At night I lay awake
in the dark and listened
to the hum in the kitchen,
the sudden start of
the refrigerator that set
the dining-room china
clattering and rang
the crystal. The curtains belled
like ballroom skirts;
a sudden snap in the floorboards,
memory of a footstep,
the belly laugh of the water heater,
a drip like Niagara Falls.

Stacy gave me a package
of stars. I peeled off the paper
backing and pressed them on the ceiling
with my palm, six flat stars

the size of my hand
and a curved moon, all
fluorescent, my own miniature
galaxy. I shone my flashlight
on them, a beam of lifeline
in the dark. Then
I switched it off
and went to sleep safe under
their glow.

Mementos

Lala's daddy brought her
a stiff doll from China and
cream-colored shells, like
knucklebones, and a pair
of lady's slippers that
we couldn't wear when we
were only four. Stacy's
brought back silk kimonos,
blood red and peach printed,
and pleated paper fans,
and wooden shoes from Holland
that only fit Jesse for about
a month. My daddy didn't
go overseas. One day
in McClellan's Dime Store
I saw colored-glass
circles and squares
and prisms on strings

that rang like chimes when
wind blew through them.
I bought them for forty cents
and hung them in my window
and at night I dreamed
of faraway places.

A Marine

Joey came back
from the war
shellshocked. He
couldn't even pour
a glass of water
his hands shook
so much. Giant trees
flew whole through the air,
he said. Islands jumped
and the noise was like
the end of the world.
He only brought back
an ashtray shaped like
Australia—a continent
he could hold in his hand
and thump to hear
a metallic ting.
He lived across the alley

behind my house with his mother,
Mrs. Van Druten, a widow, and
Australia sat empty
on the oval marble top
of a table because neither
smoked.

Age

Stacy was twelve
already—a good age to be,
it sounded so old to us. When
school started she could wear
stockings, her mother said, and
lipstick after lunch.
But Lala and I were still
eleven and would have to
wear white nylon socks with
our flat black suede shoes and
Lifebuoy-washed lips.
But that was next year
and this was still
summer and we all
went barefoot and played
outside and September
was a long time away.

Boys

Boys.
Who can explain them? Who
can understand them? They
can't even explain themselves.
They don't even try—
just do whatever they want
and let the broken bits
fall any old place. Every time
Jesse ran through our house
at least two things
would break between the front
door and the back.
He could slam doors
harder than anybody,
and he was almost two years
younger than I was. Boys're
like destructive robots. Show
them a car and they want

to take it apart the way
Jesse and Avram did my scooter
and then they couldn't put it
back again. But they didn't care
until their mothers made them
give me their life savings of
ten cents from Jesse and a dollar
from Avram.

The Attic

Stacy's grandmother built stairs
to the attic when they first
moved in with her, curving
pie-shaped steps up through
a closet, sawing
and shaping the fresh pine
lumber and nailing it
down tight, while Stacy's
father was away on a ship
during the war. He brought home
a centipede kite and hung it
at the top of the stairs so
that was the first thing
you saw when you went up,
the face with its tongue stuck
out. In some places that
is a polite greeting, he said,
instead of a hug or a kiss. But

I think he put it there because
the attic was a place for
children and the kite said,
Grownups, Keep Out!

Boys We Knew

Besides Jesse Pest,
Avram lived across the street
and Davis around the corner.
We had known them forever and
they didn't count as *boys,*
the kind we might go
on a *date* with someday,
or even want to talk to.
They were our pals, nobody
to get romantic about.
They were just like us
and didn't count.

Lefty

We called him Lefty
because he seemed made up of leftovers—
a stray, he had a thin weaseline
face, long black satiny ears
that flopped forward and backward
when he ran. He was black and
gray and white with touches
here and there of brown as though
there hadn't been enough
of one color to finish him.
He was double-jointed and
left-pawed and ran with
a rollicking rocking gallop.
But oddest of all were his
eyes. He had one blue eye, as
calm as the cloudless summer sky,
but the brown one always
had a worried look as though
it knew a dog of leftover
parts wasn't good enough.

Mary Marsden Montgomery

Kids called her
Marsh Hen and Mish Mash
and Mars Mess and Marsh Dung
and other things until
her daddy came back from France
after the war and they
shortened her name to Mimi.
What
could they have been thinking of
to name her that in the first place?

When we still played
with dolls sometimes—
because our mothers
made us when company came—Mimi
would bring a doll from her house
to spend the day. We always had
to lock up the dogs because she
was afraid of them, especially
Lefty, the sweetest gentlest

dog in the world who wouldn't
even hurt a flea when it
was biting him. We always
hid if we saw her coming and
one summer posted a Mimi lookout.
Sometimes our mothers flushed
us out of our hiding places
in the bushes and made us play all day
knowing Lefty and Bebop and Pittypat
were suffering on our back porch.
We discussed biting her ourselves
but nobody wanted to be the one
to do it.

Mimi's Feelings

Why did Mimi want
to play with us?
She only wanted to swing
or play dolls, while we
were explorers and spies
and ship captains and pirates
and treasure hunters and cowboys
and movie stars and horses. Her feelings
were hurt when you made her be *it*
and everybody ran off to hide
in the woods where we knew
she wouldn't go because she
was scared of snakes. We were, too,
but we never ever saw any
because they were more scared of us.

The Fountain in Front of the Bus Station

The fish were like chunks
of that sweet gummy orange
slice candy lying at the bottom
of the cast-iron pool. The fountain
umbrellaed over it, sparkling
spray trickled down the black iron
scrollwork and slid
into the green Jell-O water,
not even dimpling the surface.
People threw bits of trash in
to make the leaden fish move but
in that water they couldn't
if they wanted to.
I watched the still fish
and thought that maybe
at night they danced on
the rim of the fountain,
diving cleanly from its lip,

laugh bubbles trailing like
scarves behind them through
the dark water.

Robert Fisher
Northington, III

He got off the bus with
a stack of comic books in one
hand, tossing a baseball
with the other. His hair
was electric red and freckles
straggled across his face
like lost red ants. His eyes
were the color of tea. His
grin reached both ears which
stuck straight out.
You must be Rusty, my mother
said. To my embarrassment she
smothered him with a hug. He
didn't even stop tossing the ball.

Sticks and Stones

I couldn't wait to
show off my new cousin.
Stacy and Lala were waiting
on the front steps when
we got home. But
before I could introduce
them, Rusty said, Look at the bunch
of hicks from Hicksgerald,
and gave us new names.
He called Lala Lumpy and
Stacy Skatenose and I
was Deana Banana. So
we called him Crusty
and Scab and Fishhead
and Fishface and Fishbreath
and a whole lot more, but
he only laughed like
he'd been complimented.

Adoption

He was five months old,
the best baby in the Cincinnati
orphanage, a fine healthy boy
with a thatch of thick hair
the color of autumn
leaves and the brownest eyes like
a little chipmunk's that leap
with excitement when
he sees me, his new father, my uncle,
wrote home to the new grandparents.
We named him
Robert Fisher Northington, III,
and he is my son as if he sprang
from my loins, he wrote to my
mother, Rusty's new aunt and godmother.
No need to tell any
of the cousins about the adoption,
he said, but we all knew.

Eating

Rusty made fun
of everything in town.
My parents took us to eat
dinner at the Purple Duck Restaurant.
Rusty said it was lunch and called
it the Blue Goose. They took us
for supper to the Spotted Pig, famous
for cheeseburgers and banana cream pie.
He called it dinner at the Striped Hog and
ordered steak both times.

At the River

Once we went to a catfish place
that didn't have a name
on the Ocmulgee River where people
ate the whole thing with
their fingers like a piece
of fried chicken, leaving
the skeleton intact. Rusty
said that was how alley cats
eat and ordered steak instead. We
went outside when we finished while
the grownups talked. Fireflies
flashed in the Spanish moss and
the woods sang all around us.
A toad sat by the front steps waiting
for its meal to fly by.
I wanted to walk down to the river
and wade in the soft mud shallows
but Rusty wouldn't leave the circle

of light from the porch to look
at the Oakie River, as he called it.
He threw rocks at the toad
until it hopped into the spiky
palmettos that hissed with every
breeze and then he threw them at me.
They all landed short but
I went to the river and
watched the brown water slide past.
I made a boat from a slab
of bark with a leaf
sail strung on a twig
and watched it navigate
the dark water, around
the bend the river made
on its way to the sea.
Later my mother scolded me
for leaving Rusty alone,
a guest in our house and
in a strange place so far
from home. I'd rather
play with a toad, I told her.

Why

Why was Rusty so mean?
He couldn't speak to
me without sneering unless
my mother was around. He called us
hicks from Hicksgerald
at least four times a day.
Our summer equilibrium was
wrecked the minute
he stepped off that
bus. Why don't you just
go back where you came from?
we shouted. Nobody
wants you here.

Double Brains

We could hold our own
in Monopoly or Rummy or Go Fish
or Canasta but Rusty
was the champion of Double Brains.
He wouldn't play on the floor.
That's kid stuff, playing
brains on the floor,
he said. So we spread
our two decks of cards
on the New Orleans-style,
glass-topped table
on the screened porch.
We squirmed on the hard
white wrought-iron chairs with
stiff red-upholstered seats and curled
our bare toes around the bars
that ran from each table leg
to the center which held

a pot of white geraniums and played Double Brains. Each player turned over two cards as long as he could turn up pairs. Rusty always beat us but we couldn't figure out why.

Hair

Our mothers rinsed our hair
in vinegar or lemon juice
to lighten it, they said.
My mother put olive oil
on my hair every week and
made me sleep with it wrapped
in a towel. The smell
made me queasy all night.
The vinegar turned my hair
red but lemon juice made it shiny
and itchy. Stacy's mother
rolled her hair on empty
tomato juice cans. Mine used hard
metal curlers and clamps with teeth
and kid curlers that I thought
were for kids but they were really
to torture everybody with straight
hair—wire encased in soft kid

leather—they looked like brown
snap beans. The wires were always
coming through and sticking into
my scalp. Lala had naturally
curly hair but it curled
the wrong way so she got
a permanent almost
every month.

Parsley Pets

We caught caterpillars
with yellow and black stripes
in the parsley old
Mrs. Van Druten grew. They
had cute faces with
nubbinlike horns.
We called them our pets
and said we taught them
tricks. We made them leap
over twigs, never dreaming
that they were on their way
to becoming butterflies.

The Players

We had always acted out
things we read in grownup books and
magazines. That summer we
did *Gone with the Wind*.
Stacy was Scarlet and Melanie,
and Rusty was Rhett and Ashley.
Lala and I were Suellen and Careen
and Aunt Pittypat and Mammy
and Prissy. Jesse had to be
everything that nobody else was.
Avram played Sam and
Dr. Meade and Charles Hamilton
and Davis was Frank and both the Tarleton
twins. He thought they should swap
because Rusty had red hair like
the twins and his was black like Rhett's
but everybody voted him down.
All summer we acted in the attic

playroom, never minding the heat.
Sometimes we played a family.
Stacy and Rusty were the parents
and the rest of us their children.
No one argued, no one fought or
cried, and Rusty forgot to tease.
It was the most fun we'd ever had,
playing grownup.

Joey's Hobby

Joey needed something
to do. He took up woodworking
and built himself a shop
attached to the end of the garage
where he made bookcases and
bookends and boxes for everybody
he knew. That summer he moved
his things out there to live. But
at night he zipped himself into
his jungle hammock slung
from the long limb of a pecan tree
and slept with stars blooming
over him.

Getting On

Other GIs went back
to school, graduated from college,
opened businesses, got married,
started families. But Joey
stayed in his backyard and
chugged around town in his mother's
1936 black Packard doing errands
and puttering about. One day
he drove to the train station
and left the Packard keys
with the stationmaster.
Joey's mother walked a half
mile to drive the Packard home.
Joey had left on the southbound
train. His hammock was gone
from the tree. We imagined
wild adventures, Joey hunting
gold in Africa, butterflies in Peru,

growing rubber in Borneo, all
places where he could sling his jungle
hammock and swing gently from a tree.
But he'd only gone to the coast
where he was a druggist in Brunswick,
his mother said.

Painted Lady

Joey married Vivian Malone
and brought her to Fitzgerald
to meet his mother. He found
her in Brunswick, a nurse,
he said, at the VA hospital.
Under a streetlight,
our mothers said with a wink. No,
we explained, Joey said
they met at a party. We thought
Vivian looked like she
went to a party every night
even in the daytime. Her hair
was a swirl of auburn with
a life of its own, like
leaves in an autumn wind,
her skin pale as pearl,
big glass-green eyes with
cinnamon lashes. She always smiled

and wore green, ankle-strap,
high-heeled shoes. We all
wanted to look like Vivian Malone.

Earrings

Our mothers wore round
or square earbobs that
clipped like knots
to their earlobes and
twisted metal knobs that looked
like they hurt a lot.
Vivian wore big dangling
gold hoops that swung
when she walked
and shimmered when she laughed,
with a tinkly sound.

The Newcomer

She could crack
her gum like a Spanish
dancer's castanets
in the movies. Call me Viv,
she said through Flame Kiss
lips when our mothers
invited her over for
a CoCola. They had planned
to give her a welcoming
party but for some reason
changed their minds.

Afraid

Rusty wouldn't swim to the deep
end of the pool and he batted away
the little silvery fish that nibbled at
us in the clear water of Oswichee Spring.
They don't bite, we told him,
they only tickle. But he didn't
believe us so we told him
about the spring caverns that went
to the middle of the earth and
he wouldn't swim across that
even though we explained
that the water pumped upward
so you couldn't get sucked in
the way we had thought when
we were little and didn't know
any better. He wouldn't jump into the hay
from Stacy's uncle's loft which was
perfectly safe—not even Jesse

had ever broken any bones doing it—
and he wouldn't ride Maud the
plowhorse who loved peppermint sticks
or my pony Rocky who ate pickles and
cereal with milk out of a bowl.
He wouldn't even go barefoot
like the rest of us and
told us that hicks
from Hicksgerald had worms.

Small Revenge

Rusty made the hatefulist
remarks. He said
I looked like a pot sticker.
Nobody knew what that was
until Vivian explained it
was a Chinese dumpling.
He called Stacy noodlehead
and Lala sauerkrautbrains.
Our meals were farm food
to him but I noticed
his plate was always empty
when he left the table.
He liked city food, he said,
foreign and spicy and hot.
We can cook like that, we
said, and we made him
a southern barbecue sandwich
drenched with hot

mustard and horseradish and
Tabasco sauce and sprinkled
with red and black pepper.
He ate the whole thing, said
it was delicious, at least
you can make a decent sandwich,
but a few minutes later we
saw him in the backyard
hosing out his mouth
for ten minutes. He
didn't talk much about
food after that.

Nightsounds

Crickets and frogs screeched
for hours in the woods and
swamp a block away.
At eleven the southbound
train blew its whistle to
clear the tracks. Sometimes
a screech owl answered. I
could hear a car for a half-mile
before and after it passed my house.
Wind teased the pear
leaves and set them whispering
like gossips in the dark.
But that summer I heard
a new sound like a small
animal or a bird trapped
somewhere in the attic.
It could be a rat, Lala
said, or a bat Stacy suggested.

With a flick of the switch
the attic fan roared through
the house scouring all sounds
but sometimes I could hear
the small animal cry over
the rushing sea.

The Green Turnip

Rusty left the lamp on
all night. I fell asleep
reading comics, he said.
My mother pulled down
the disappearing stairs
to the attic and got
my old dog lamp,
a cocker spaniel with a blue
bulb like a ball in its mouth.
Only the blue bulb was burned out so
she put a pointed green Christmas
bulb in. The dog looked like
it was eating a green turnip.
When the lights were out
a greenish glow crept down the hall.
Once when I went half asleep to
the bathroom, I thought Martians
were in the guest room. Then
I remembered it was
only Rusty.

Hummingbird

Hovering
in the hedge
where summer
flowers bloomed like
tiny scarlet bells,
a thin bird's beak
sipped nectar
while a fizz of wings
kept it in place.

Learning to Swim

We swam in the baby
pool, water wings sprouting
from underarm straps
until we were six and
had lessons from my neighbor
Bayard, a high school
senior. Our mothers
drove us ten miles
and we made up the famous
rhyme: around the curve
and down the hill and
here we are at Bowen's Mill,
and later everyone chanted it
when they went swimming
at the Bowen's Mill pool.
That first morning Lala
looked up at Bayard and
said, Ain't he cute!

We were all secretly
in love with him but
he belonged to Daphne across
the street from me.
She courted him with her
music, playing the piano and singing
with her front door open
so he would be sure to
hear her while he mowed
the lawn or trimmed the hedge.
Once we all lined up
at my front door and howled
to drown Daphne out. Our
mothers came running, certain
that we were in the direst trouble.
Daphne's music worked because she
and Bayard got married when they
graduated from college.
For a long time after
we thought that was how you
got boys to marry
you—by singing
with your front door open.

The Town

One rainy day
Rusty said let's
build a town. We collected
boxes and paper and scraps from
my mother's sewing machine drawers.
All morning we cut and crayoned
and pasted houses and buildings,
even a tiny bus station, a fountain
in front made from jar lids
with orange peel fish floating
in real water. We drove Rusty's fleet
of little cars, trucks, taxis, and buses up
and down the streets of our miniature
Fitzgerald and not once did Rusty
call it Hicksgerald.

The Party

For Rusty's thirteenth birthday
the grownups borrowed Cecil Stubbs'
flatbed truck loaded
with bales of hay from Stacy's
uncle and took a group
of kids his age and Avram,
Lala, Stacy, and me
to Bowen's Mill where we
swam all afternoon
and roasted hotdogs and
walked down to the old
wooden dam on the millpond.
We dodged horseflies and
mosquitoes and when we
got to the dam it was too dark
to see anything anyway.

The Girls

At the party
the girls danced the shag
in sets like square
dancers to endless
boogie-woogie and
"Sweet Georgia Brown,"
while the boys took turns
jumping out of the open
windows of the pavilion and
hanging around the bowling
alley next door and
the shooting gallery outside
until the grownups made
them go back inside. We
stared across the dance floor
at them until somebody
played "Ain't She Sweet"
and Fletcher Fuller asked

Mimi to dance. She flipped
her long hair and they shagged
like a floor show until Avram's
brother cut in. After that
everybody started dancing in couples
except Lala and Stacy and me.

The Panther
on the Rampage

The grownups rounded
up the party. Back on the truck,
they ordered. There's
a panther in the woods.
Panther!
Everyone screamed and yelled and
stared into the dark all around us,
wanting to be the first
to see it stalking
through the palmettos
and pines. Every car
had panther eyes, its growl
roared in the trees.
I see it! Mimi shrieked,
terrible red eyes getting
closer. Where?
Just ahead. But it
was only the taillights

of a car. There were at
least fourteen sightings before
we got to the safety of
town lights.

Truth

The night was pantherine.
We could see the shine
of its coat, the awful curve
of its fangs, the red
gleam of its eyes in
a thousand trees arching
and leaping out of the darkness
around us.
But
I'd heard the grownups whisper—
the panther was really a convict
escaped during transport.
A convict! everyone
shrieked louder.
But it was the panther
we all saw in the dark,
in our dreams, and panther
eyes that watched us then.

Party Continued

The party went back to my house
where the rug was rolled back
in the living room and Rusty
danced every time with Mimi.
Drastic action was clearly
called for. Lala and I sent Stacy
home for her black satin
gypsy skirt. We made her take
her braids down to turn her
straight hair into a wavy
mane. Her white peasant blouse would do
but she needed something more.
With long black shoelaces we
turned her ballet shoes into
ankle straps and pinned
a rose in her hair
with a crisscross
of bobby pins. But the best

came from the old tube of
lipstick Vivian had
given us. We carefully
outlined Stacy's mouth and
suddenly Lala and I backed away
to look at this stranger
with Flame Kiss lips.

The Trade

We bribed Davis
to dance with Stacy,
offering him all our comics.
He said he'd read them but
he'd do it for my microscope.
That was too much and he knew it.
I wouldn't be able to look at
hairs and scabs and dirt
and things. So I offered
my next best treasure: a skeleton
about a foot tall made of plastic
that a pharmaceutical salesman
had given my father. OK,
Davis said, bones for bones.
They bounced around the floor
to "A Bushel and a Peck,"
until Fletcher Fuller broke
in and Rusty noticed and
asked Stacy to dance.

The Party Outside

My mother shooed some of us
outside, Lala and Avram and me.
Jesse was watching for us
from his window. He climbed out
and ran over in his short-pants
pj's printed with red airplanes.
We held hands under the string
of colored lights that
bisected the backyard and
danced the shag in a circle
on the dew-slick grass.
The pear tree spurted over us
like a green fountain, its leaves
shimmering against the globed lights
red, yellow, purple, and blue as
we spun to the music. Somewhere
above us stars and planets
and comets and moons were
shining their hearts out.

The Next Day

How was it, we could hardly
wait to ask. Stacy didn't seem
to know what we meant. Dancing
with Rusty we said. Like
dancing with Jesse, she said,
only taller. She wouldn't
tell us if Rusty kissed her.
Lala and I had endless
discussions of the subject.
But Stacy would only smile.
We consulted Vivian. She
said it was Stacy's
secret. It wasn't fair.
Stacy had crossed a line
that we hadn't even known
was there. Lala and I
lay under the pear tree
and watched the passing clouds
and wondered when
our turn would come.

Crimson Wings

Vivian Van Druten got
a job at the hospital
proving that she really
was a nurse. Nobody
in the movies had ever
looked as glamorous
as Vivian in her crisp
white uniform, her cap
anchored like a galleon
on her frothy red hair,
her navy cape flung back
so that the silk lining
showed like crimson wings
across her shoulders.

Cheating

Rusty dropped a lot
of cards when we played Double
Brains on the glass-topped table.
One day I dropped a card and
found out why he always beat us.
I could see the faces
of all the cards from underneath.
I didn't tell but
we made a new rule. If
a card got dropped,
you lost your turn. After
that Rusty didn't drop
his cards anymore and
he didn't win all the time
either.

The Secret

Something woke me,
not the chime or a dream or
cars lights or panther eyes.
I padded barefoot following
the sounds up the hall
to the guest room
where I listened outside
the door with the line of light
under it. I heard someone
crying but nobody was
in there except Rusty. What
did he have to cry about?
He was on vacation and
had a new baby sister
waiting for him at home like
a surprise he'd never seen.
I wished I had one or
even a brother. I tiptoed back

to my room where I
watched the stars glowing
on my ceiling until they
faded and I went to sleep.
I could have burst into his
room and laughed at him.
I could have teased him
the rest of the summer
like he did me but I
never told Lala or Stacy.
I never even told Rusty,
that I knew.

The Letter

My mother got a letter
from Aunt Celia. She said
Rusty had had a good time
on his visit.
He wrote an account
for his school paper,
all about his summer in a country
called Fitzgerald, deep in the
bottom of nowhere and listed
all the things he did like
riding a stallion and exploring
underwater caves and jumping
off housetops and how he fought off
a wild panther and saw a convict
get arrested. That boy
has a lot of imagination,
my mother said. He'd better
stick to fiction, she wrote
Aunt Celia back.

A New Profession

Joey Van Druten turned
his workshop into an aviary.
Where once carpenter's tools
hung on the rough board
walls, now sunlight dappled
the vines that climbed
to the skylight he cut
into the roof and
the parakeets he raised
flitted by on pastel wings,
like broken-off bits
of blue sky and flying flowers
in their new jungle-walled home
adding their notes to
summer's song.

August

The pears were gone, bottled
in glass jars as piquant
relish or amberous
preserves to perk up winter meals.
Rotten pears were raked away
with the long green tendrils
of St. Augustine grass and dropped
in the horse pasture. Lala and I lay
in the pear tree shade waiting
for Stacy shopping uptown for
high school clothes. Summer
seemed to be racing toward
September but we tried to
hold on to its last moments.
It would be strange, we said,
going to Third Ward Elementary
without Stacy where she
had showed us our classroom that

first day six years ago.
A girl crossed the tar line
on the sidewalk, a tall girl
in a straight plaid skirt and
red sweater, her hair in the latest
poodle cut, shiny new pennies
winking from the slots of her brown
loafers. Stacy. We stared
as she turned up the
alley to Mimi's house first
to show off her school clothes.
Stunned, we waited until
she came back to let us
see her new look and we knew
summer was finally over.

FRANKLIN PIERCE COLLEGE LIBRARY

00110571

DATE DUE

APR 2 0 2008			
GAYLORD			PRINTED IN U.S.A.